KT-217-333

Changing Charlie

Scoular Anderson

Collins

This edition produced for The Book People Ltd
Hall Wood Avenue, Haydock
St Helens WA11 9UL

Published by A & C Black in 1992
Published by Collins in 1993
10 9 8 7 6
Collins an imprint of HarperCollins*Publishers* Ltd,
77-85 Fulham Palace Road, Hammersmith, London W6 8JB.

ISBN 0 00 763092 1

Text and illustrations © Scoular Anderson 1992

Scoular Anderson asserts the moral right to
be identified as the author/illustrator of the work.
A CIP record for this title is available from the British Library.

Printed and bound in Great Britain by
Omnia Books Limited, Glasgow

All rights reserved. No part of this publication mat be reproduced, stored in a retrieval system,
or transmitted in any form or by any means, electronic, mechanical, photocopying, recording
or otherwise, without the prior permission of HarperCollins*Publishers* Ltd,
77-85 Fulham Palace Road, Hammersmith, London W6 8JB.

CHAPTER 1 Ho-Ho-Ho!

Charlie was very good at
making faces.

Each time he passed the mirror in
the hall, he stopped to do an
impression.

He could make his face fat,

and he
could make
it thin.

He could make
his face round
and small like
Miss Twill
next door.

He could make
himself jolly
and full of teeth
like Mr Rinzal in
the corner shop.

He could go as red as a beetroot
or as white as a sheet just by
thinking about it.

And the more faces he made,
the better they were.

CHAPTER 2 Miaoow!

One day, he decided to pull his best face ever. He wanted to make himself look like a cat.

He stood in front of the mirror, held his breath and thought very hard.

He thought about pointy ears . . .

. . . and stripy fur.

He was just thinking about a little
pink nose

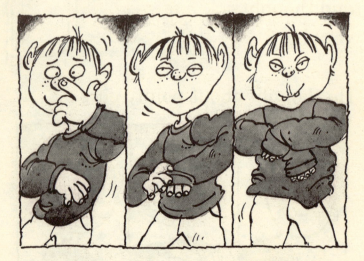

when his mum came into the hall.

Charlie turned and said very loudly,

His mum was so scared that she ran out of the door, yelling

Soon she came charging back in,
with a brush to chase the cat away,

but she was too late. By that time,
Charlie had stopped being a cat.

Charlie was very pleased with his animal impressions. He wanted to try some more.

So he went
to the pet
shop on the
corner.

He stared in the window and
wondered if he should be a goldfish

or a budgie,

or a hamster.

In the end, he decided to be a
spotty puppy.

It must have been
a good impression,
because the puppy
in the window
began to bark.

YAP!

Then something odd happened . . .

CHAPTER 3 SCREECH!

A van pulled up
behind Charlie
and a nasty-looking
boy jumped out.
Charlie knew
him from school.
It was Dexter
Clogpot.

But Dexter didn't know Charlie.
He ran over and grabbed Charlie by
the waist.

Before Charlie could do anything, he
was dumped in the back of the van.

The door was shut and the van
drove off.

Charlie got to his feet. He was
just able to peep through the
window into the cab.

He could see Dexter and his older brother, Bernie. Together, they were nothing but trouble.

They had an older sister called Rosabella who was even worse. Charlie hoped this had nothing to do with her.

16

THE SKILMUGGLIE GRAND SUMMER FÊTE

PRIZES FOR HOME-GROWN FRUIT, VEGETABLES & FLOWERS, BAKING AND JAM-MAKING

Gymnastic displays and dancing by the Skilmugglie Majorettes

PLUS

THE PROUD PUP DOG SHOW

THE CUP WILL BE PRESENTED BY LADY MARCIA BEESWING

Charlie didn't know what to do.
His impression had been so good
that Dexter thought he had
kidnapped a real dog.

What would happen when the Clogpots
found they didn't have a spotty
puppy after all?

CHAPTER 4 AAAGH!

At last the van stopped and Bernie opened the back door.

He quickly slammed it shut again.

Dexter opened the back of the van and peered in. He saw something very hairy and very fierce.

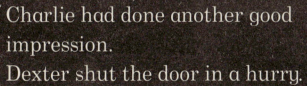

Charlie had done another good impression.

Dexter shut the door in a hurry.

24

CHAPTER **5** AAEEEE!

At that moment Rosabella came out of the house dressed up for the fête.

Before they could stop her, she had
opened the back of the van.
Bernie twitched. Dexter gulped.

There was a horrible

Rosabella was furious.

Bernie and Dexter peered over
her shoulder.

Sure enough, the van was empty, apart from an old cardboard box in the corner. Charlie's impressions were getting better and better.

'That's it!' said Rosabella.
She had thought of a cunning plan.

Blinko was thrown into the back of the van with Charlie. He didn't look too friendly, so Charlie did another impression.

Blinko shrank into a corner and stayed there until the van drew up at the fête.

Charlie didn't want to be seen by the Clogpots, and there was only one way to escape.

He would pretend to be Blinko.

When the door was opened, he was ready . . .

. . . to leap out and run for it.

But he wasn't quick enough.
As soon as the door opened,
a dog lead was slipped around
his neck.

Dexter lifted him out of the van.

And Rosabella was waiting for him.

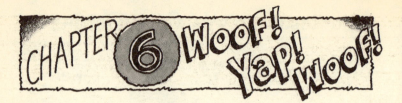

Things were getting tricky for Charlie. He had to keep looking like Blinko, or he would be in trouble.

But it was difficult crawling along the ground like a dog.

As Charlie entered the show-ring,
the dogs began to sniff
suspiciously at him.

Charlie wanted to get away.
He tried to run but Rosabella
held on tightly to the lead.

Soon, the whole place was in an
uproar. Charlie couldn't pretend
to be a dog any more.

One of the judges spotted him
right away.

Rosabella just stood and stared.
She couldn't believe her eyes.

Charlie saw
his chance.
He slipped
off the lead
and ran.

CHAPTER 7 KERRASH!

Charlie ran out of the show-ring and
headed for the big tent.
He lifted a corner of the canvas . . .

. . . and squeezed underneath.
Inside the tent were long tables,
loaded with prize vegetables,
pots of jam and flowers.

And on the top table sat the
Proud Pup Dog Show Cup.

Charlie was wondering what he should do next, when Bernie and Dexter came rushing into the tent.

They seemed to be very interested in the things on the tables.

49

So that was what they were up to!

Suddenly, Bernie snatched a plate of prize apples and ran for the door.

Charlie felt he had been in enough
trouble for one day, but he didn't
want the Clogpots to get their
hands on the cup.

The guard ran outside, and Dexter
made a dash for the cup.

But he
wasn't
looking
where
he was
going.

KERRASH!

While Dexter dug himself out from
under a pile of prize vegetables
and strawberry jam,

Charlie had just enough time to
sneak down to the end of the tent.
He grabbed the cup and hid it under
the table.

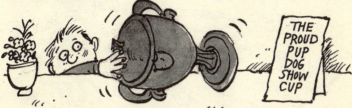

Then he jumped on to the table.
He started to think about
sticky-out-handles
and a shiny face . . .

. . . he was just in time.

Dexter picked him up

and carried him back to the van,
where Bernie was waiting.

Just then, Rosabella came back.

They jumped into the van
and roared off.

When they got home, Bernie opened
the van with a smug smile
on his face.

Dexter and Bernie peered inside.
There was nothing there
but a very bad-tempered Blinko –
and that old box.

59

Rosabella was not pleased.

Dexter and Bernie began to run,
but she was just behind them.

At last, Charlie
saw his chance
to escape.

CHAPTER 9 GRRRRR!

When Charlie reached home,
his mum didn't seem very pleased
to see him.

On the way up to the bathroom, Charlie stopped in front of the mirror . . .

. . . but his mum put her head round the kitchen door.

Later on, she came to pick up Charlie's dirty clothes for the washing machine. It's just as well she didn't look in the shower . . .

Charlie was doing one last impression.

Tomorrow he would just be himself.